I read this book all by myself

....

For Abbi and Daniel – AM
For Dylan and Hatti – KB

MAGIC MR EDISON
A Red Fox Book: 0 09 943418 0

First published in Great Britain in 2002 by Red Fox
an imprint of Random House Children's Books

3 5 7 9 10 8 6 4 2

Text copyright © Andrew Melrose 2002
Illustrations copyright © Katja Bandlow 2002

Set in Cheltenham Book Infant

Red Fox Books are published by Random House Children's Books,
61–63 Uxbridge Road, London W5 5SA,
a division of The Random House Group Ltd,
in Australia by Random House Australia (Pty) Ltd,
20 Alfred Street, Milsons Point, Sydney, NSW 2061, Australia,
in New Zealand by Random House New Zealand Ltd,
18 Poland Road, Glenfield, Auckland 10, New Zealand,
and in South Africa by Random House (Pty) Ltd,
Endulini, 5A Jubilee Road, Parktown 2193, South Africa

THE RANDOM HOUSE GROUP Limited Reg. No. 954009

www.kidsatrandomhouse.co.uk

A CIP catalogue record for this book is available from the British Library.

Printed and bound in Singapore by Tien Wah Press

Magic Mr Edison

Andrew Melrose   Katja Bandlow

RED FOX

AMERICA 1879

Dan waved goodbye to his grandma and set off home. "Look, Charlie," he said to his pup, "the sun is setting already. We'll have to hurry."

Dan waved to the lamplighter.

"You're going home late tonight, Dan," he said.

"I had to fetch more coal for Grandma's fire. She gets cold on these dark winter nights," said Dan.

Charlie growled as the lamplighter waved his stick in the air.

"Oh, Charlie," said Dan, "he's only trying to make the street brighter for us! Come on, it's home time."

Dan and Charlie waited to cross the road. The street lamp flickered and turned on. Charlie growled at the dark jumpy shadows.

"Don't worry, Charlie," said Dan. "We'll soon be home. We can take the short cut through the park. Big Moon is out tonight. He'll give us plenty of light!"

Charlie barked up at the moon. Dan laughed. But suddenly a rattling tramcar came rumbling by. The noise frightened Charlie so much, he yelped and ran off.

"Charlie!" shouted Dan. "Charlie, come back!"

Charlie disappeared into the park. Dan chased after him.

In the park, Big Moon smiled down at
Dan. But Dan was too sad to smile back.
He had lost Charlie and it was getting
dark. Dan didn't like the dark. Or being
alone in the park.

"Charlie!" he shouted again.

Dan tiptoed through the park, looking in all their favourite places – down by the old tree, under the bushes and down by the pond. But it was no use.

Suddenly, Charlie ran out from behind the bandstand. Dan got such a fright, he screamed!

Charlie got such a fright, he ran away again.

Woof!

"Charlie! Come back!" shouted Dan.
Charlie usually did what he was told,
but not today.
"He must really be scared," thought
Dan. "I have to catch him!"

Out on the street, Charlie ran straight
into the lamplighter.

Dan wove in and out of the crowd calling his pup's name.

Charlie knocked over a fruit cart. Apples and pears rolled everywhere.

"Oh, Charlie!" said Dan.

Then something terrible happened.

A man bent down to pick up Charlie.

"Well now, little scruff," said the man, "are you lost?"

The man took Charlie into a tall building. Dan didn't know what to do. He had to rescue Charlie!

He followed the man into the building.

Inside, it was very dark. Dan heard strange clanking noises. He tiptoed forward. A long scary shadow stretched down the hall in front of him.

"Charlie!" Dan whispered softly. "Charlie, where are you?"

No one answered.

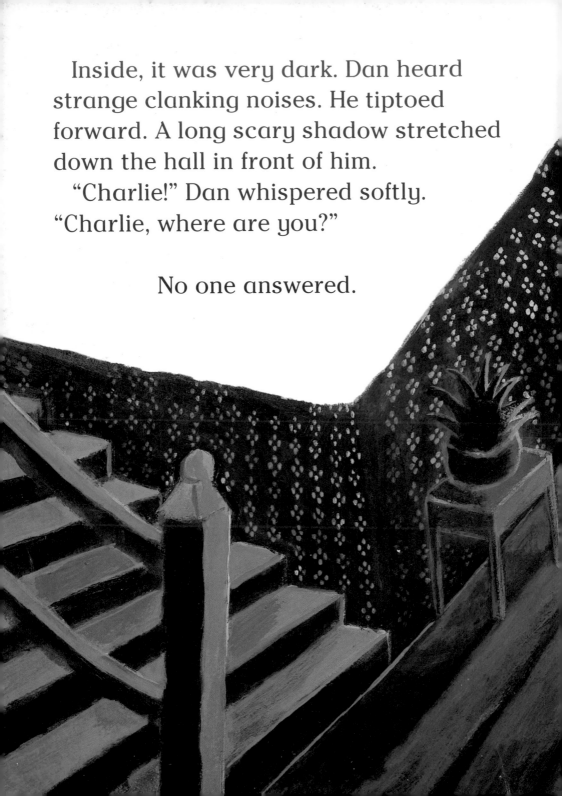

Dan opened the door into a long, dark room. Something ran between his legs. It made Dan jump.

"Charlie," he whispered, loudly, "is that you?"

No one answered.

"I wish I had a candle," Dan said. He didn't like the dark or the shadows, and he was beginning to think he would never see Charlie again.

"Why do you need a candle?"
asked a loud voice behind him.
Dan shouted out in surprise.
Charlie hid under a table.

Dan looked up at the man with the loud voice. "Sorry, mister," he said. "I didn't mean to be here. I just came to get Charlie."

"So he's your pup, is he?" said the man. "Here, come and push this switch for me."

Dan was so scared he was shaking. But he did as he was told.

Suddenly, a bright light filled the room.

"That's better," said the man. "Now I can see you both."

Even Charlie came out to have a look.
"Look, Charlie, it's light everywhere!"
said Dan.

"Not just any light," said the man. "It's electric light!"

"Is it magic?" asked Dan.

The man with the loud voice laughed. "Oh, no. It's not magic, it's science."

"Does that mean you are a scientist?" asked Dan.

"That's right," said the man. "My name is Thomas Edison."

"Mr Edison," said Dan, "did you make this electric light?"

"I sure did," said Edison.

"Wow!" said Dan.

"All you need to make light is a battery that makes electricity. Then you attach some wire and a light bulb like this."

Mr Edison showed Dan the bulb.
"It is just a bubble made out of glass with
a piece of wire inside. The electricity
heats up the wire and that makes the
light shine."

"Wow!" said Dan again. "I don't like the dark. But tonight Charlie and I had to walk home in it. When it's dark, we need Big Moon to light our way. But sometimes, when it's cloudy, we can't even see Big Moon."

"Well," said Mr Edison, "some day there will be electric light everywhere. Then, when it gets dark, you will be able to just switch it on whenever you like."

"Now, you'd better get on home, or your mother will be worried," said Mr Edison.

Dan nodded. "Thank you for showing Charlie and me your electric light, Mr Edison," said Dan.

"Come back and see it any time you like!" said Mr Edison.

When Dan got outside, he stopped and looked up at Big Moon. "Oh, Charlie, won't it be magic when we can switch on the light of a big moon any time we like?"

The lamp uses mains electricity for power.

A light bulb is a glass bulb with a thin metal wire inside. When electricity from a battery or the mains goes through the wire, it makes it hot so it gives off light.

Thomas Edison (1847–1931) was born in Ohio, USA. He grew up to be a great inventor. In 1879 he invented the first light bulb. Three years later, he lit up a whole neighbourhood of New York City. People were very excited to have electric light on the streets and in their homes. Edison also invented the phonograph, which could record and play back music, like CDs today.

45

Andrew Melrose

Where did you get the idea for this story? One day I was looking up at the light, and I wondered who invented it. When I discovered it was Thomas Edison I decided to write a story about him.

How long did it take to write this story? It took a few hours to write a rough draft, then a much longer time to do what we call editing. Editing is what you do when you want to change the words, or the story or even the spellings.

Is Edison your favourite inventor? Yes, because he also invented the first phonograph, which was like the first tape recorder or CD player. I like listening to music very much.

Have times changed much since you were a child? Not half! We have central heating in my house, but when I was little all we had was a coal fire. We didn't have a telephone either, or a fridge.

What did you like to do when you were a child? What did you hate? I liked playing football, reading and playing my guitar. I didn't like homework or delivering newspapers on cold mornings – oh, and I hated having baths.

Katja Bandlow

Meet the illustrator.

What did you use to paint the pictures in this book?
I painted the pictures with dry acrylic paints. There are loads of layers underneath the one you can see, so the picture takes shape slowly, until I decide it's finished. I painted all the pictures at the same time. It took me three months to paint the whole book.

What's your favourite place to draw? My desk is my favourite place to draw. It is cosy, with music and fresh flowers. I also love doodling figures and animals, so I take a little notebook everywhere I go.

Where do you live? I live in Hamburg, Germany.

Did you draw when you were a child? Yes, loads. We only go to school half-days in Germany. I used to lie on the floor and paint all afternoon listening to records with my friends.

What did you like to do when you were a child? I loved going to the sweet shop, playing outside and painting.

Will you try and write or draw a story too?

Let your ideas take flight with

Flying Foxes

Slow Magic
by Pippa Goodhart and John Kelly

Magic Mr Edison
by Andrew Melrose and Katja Bandlow

Only Tadpoles Have Tails
by Jane Clarke and Jane Gray

That's Not Right!
by Alan Durant and Katharine McEwen

Don't Let the Bad Bugs Bite!
by Lindsey Gardiner

A Tale of Two Wolves
by Susan Kelly and Lizzie Finlay

All the Little Ones – and a Half
by Mary Murphy

Sherman Swaps Shells
by Jane Clarke and Ant Parker

Digging for Dinosaurs
by Judy Waite and Garry Parsons

Shadowhog
by Sandra Ann Horn and Mary McQuillan

The Magic Backpack
by Julia Jarman and Adriano Gon

Jake and the Red Bird
by Ragnhild Scamell and Valeria Petrone